Emily Snape

BuSy LizZie
Family Forever

WACKY BEE

Published by
Wacky Bee Books
Riverbank House, 1 Putney Bridge Approach, London SW6 3JD

ISBN: 978-1-913292-63-8

First published in the UK, 2023

Text and illustrations © Emily Snape, 2023

Design by David Rose

Printed and bound by Akcent Media

www.wackybeebooks.com

Contents

BuSy LizZie

and the Sweetie Stash

Lizzie hopped excitedly from one foot to the other.

'Do you need a wee or something?' Isaac snorted while plunging his bread soldier head first into his boiled egg and exploding bright yellow yolk all over his plate.

'Or have you got ants in your pants?' asked Milo, scooping up a forkful of baked beans.

Lizzie didn't react. That was usually the best way when dealing with her big brothers. Especially as they were twins, which made them double-trouble. She didn't even CONSIDER throwing her egg at them. There was already too much going on in her brain. She was busily trying to work out EXACTLY how many hours were left until her birthday officially began. She'd started counting down almost as soon as her last birthday was over. And that was 364 long days ago. Now, AT LAST, it was her birthday eve!

She studied the minute hand on the kitchen clock as it swung around to 7 p.m.

'In only FIVE HOURS,' said Lizzie, still

hopping up and down. 'Only FIVE HOURS until my birthday fun can finally begin!'

'It'll be midnight in five hours,' said Milo, rolling his eyes. 'You won't be celebrating your birthday. You'll be sucking your thumb, fast asleep.'

'No, I won't!' said Lizzie. 'And I don't suck my thumb, thank you very much. I'm going to start celebrating my birthday the EXACT moment I turn eight.'

'There's NO WAY you'll be able to stay awake till 12 o'clock!' said Isaac, crossing his arms.

'Yes, I will. You'll see,' said Lizzie, sticking out her bottom lip.

'OK! Well, here's a challenge,' said Milo.

'You have to give us half your birthday money if you're not awake at midnight, and... er...'

'...YOU have to hand over your ENTIRE secret stash of sweets if I am!' interrupted Lizzie quickly.

Lizzie had known for ages that her brothers had a secret sweetie stash. She kept spotting them nibbling gummy snakes or blowing great big bubblegum bubbles when Mum wasn't looking. And they wouldn't share ANY of their sweets with her.

Their mum didn't allow sweets in the house. She was a yoga teacher and took healthy eating, early bedtimes and regular exercise VERY seriously. The children were only allowed jam on special occasions, and the boys would be in BIG TROUBLE if their sweetie haul was discovered. That's how Lizzie knew it must be hidden somewhere REALLY hard to find.

And she'd searched EVERYWHERE.
She'd even dared to look under the boys'
bunk bed and risked getting her hand
nibbled by a cheesy sock-monster.
But she'd had
no luck.

'Fine,' agreed Isaac, already planning what to spend HIS half of the cash on.

'You're on,' added Milo. 'You'll have to come into our room at one minute past midnight to prove you're awake!'

Milo winked at Isaac and grinned.

'And if you don't, that money is ours!' said Isaac.

'See you at 12.01,' said Lizzie, pushing past her brothers and marching confidently upstairs to her bedroom.

She wasn't worried. Of COURSE she could stay awake till midnight. How hard could it be?

Unfortunately, things weren't going Lizzie's way. First of all, her mum read her a VERY long and VERY dull bedtime story about an incredibly slow snail who kept getting lost up a mountain. Lizzie's eyelids were beginning to feel SO heavy that it was almost impossible to keep them open. It was as if tiny pixies were pulling them closed.

Eventually,
her mum
whispered, 'Goodnight,
nearly-birthday girl', turned off
the light and crept out of the room.

Lizzie slowly counted to ten, then she leaped out of bed and switched on her lamp. She did twenty star jumps, two roly-polies, then attempted a handstand (which was actually quite tricky). Lizzie crash-landed into a pile of books, making an enormous CLATTER.

'Are you all right up there?' Mum called from downstairs.

'Er... yep. Just been to the toilet,' Lizzie called back, and hastily shoved the cascade of books into a corner.

'Surely it must be nearly midnight by now,' she thought, and gleefully checked her watch.

It was ONLY 8.37 p.m.

So, Lizzie made up a dance. Then she jumped up and down on her bed. But after a while, she began to feel sleepy again, so she started tidying up the books which she'd shoved into the corner. After that, she dug out some paper and drew a picture of a werewolf.

She looked at her watch again. It was 8.42 p.m. WAS SHE IN A TIME WARP? How could only five minutes have passed?

Lizzie stared at her bed longingly. It looked so soft and welcoming.

'NO!' she told herself sternly and decided it was time for the emergency SNACK.

Lizzie had sneaked a packet of raisins (or squashed flies as Milo called them) into her doll's house a few weeks ago for an extremely serious situation just like this. She quietly lifted the creaky, wooden roof and was just about to fish them out when she spotted something scuttling towards her wardrobe.

It was a SPIDER!

It was a top-secret fact that Lizzie was absolutely terrified of spiders. She knew, of course (because her brothers loved reminding her), that spiders were completely harmless. She knew that they were minuscule and more frightened of her than she was of them. She knew that they were VERY GOOD FOR THE ENVIRONMENT and that she should just ignore them. But she couldn't. She just couldn't. Something about spiders made her feel icky and sticky and yucky.

Lizzie leaped onto her bed and began to panic. She couldn't call for Mum. Isaac and Milo would hear her and they would tease her for WEEKS if they knew she was scared of a teeny, tiny spider. Plus, they'd accuse her of just doing it so that Mum would allow her downstairs where she might be allowed to watch the TV TO TAKE HER MIND OFF THINGS, but which would also help keep her awake. And then they'd accuse her of cheating and wouldn't let her have their sweetie stash anyway.

So, what should she do?

'Be brave, be brave,' Lizzie told herself.

Then it suddenly struck her. THE RAISINS!

Without taking her eyes off the SPIDER, she dashed to the other side of the room, fumbled around in the doll's house roof until she found the box of raisins, then scurried back to bed.

This was her plan.

She would create a trail of treats all the way to the doll's house. The spider wouldn't be able to resist. The raisins basically looked like trampled flies, and that was a spider's dream dinner, wasn't it? Then, once the spider was safely INSIDE the doll's house, Lizzie could replace the roof, and her bedroom would be creepy-crawly-free.

Lizzie quickly placed the raisins in a neat row, leading directly from the top of

the doll's house, down the little staircase
and to as close as she dared to the
spider, who continued to stay as still as a
statue. Now she just had to wait.

The spider didn't move.

'Come on, Mr Spider. They're delicious,' she whispered, as enthusiastically as she dared.

The spider didn't jerk a single stringy leg.

How could she make the raisins look more tempting? Lizzie, with one eye still on the spider, grabbed her scissors and cut out some tiny paper wings, then popped them onto the top of the raisins.

Lizzie leaped back into bed and willed the spider to move.

He didn't flinch.

Perhaps he'd go for them if he thought another spider was going to gobble them up first. So, she scrambled to her cupboard and dug around at the bottom until she found the black string she'd been saving for ages. She scrunched it up into a messy ball, then pulled a few bits loose for legs. Lizzie held it up for inspection. It SORT of looked like a giant, greedy spider. SORT of!

But when Lizzie looked back, the real spider had VANISHED. Where had he gone? She glanced frantically around, scanning for any movement. Then she spotted a skinny black leg disappearing into the doll's house.

Lizzie crept forward and, keeping as much distance between herself and the spider as she possibly could, stretched her arm out and flipped down the doll's house roof. Phew!

She felt utter relief wash over her as she climbed into bed and drew her lovely, warm covers over her shoulders. With the spider safely out of the way, she could finally concentrate properly on staying awake.

It was hours later when Lizzie felt a tickle on her cheek. She popped open her eyes and saw the little spider right on the tip of her nose.

Lizzie froze. The spider stayed perfectly still. A chill crept up her spine. Without moving, she peered around, unsure what to do. And that's when she realised... she'd been asleep in bed. It was her ACTUAL birthday, and she suddenly remembered all about THE CHALLENGE and THE SWEETIE STASH... and that she needed to be wide awake at MIDNIGHT.

Lizzie brushed the spider onto her pillow as carefully as she could and looked at her watch. It was exactly midnight. She couldn't quite believe it. She blinked and checked again. The spider must have found his way out of the doll's house and woken her up. She could kiss him! (But she didn't.) She thanked the spider politely and promised to give him a fizzy cola bottle later. Then she tip-toed directly into her brothers' room. She could hear Isaac and Milo both snoring softly. She eagerly shook Milo's arm.

'Huh?' he croaked, confused.

'It's five minutes past midnight,' she whispered.

'What's going on?' said Isaac, peering over the edge of the top bunk. He sleepily rubbed his eyes and looked at the clock on the wall.

'Hey, it is,' he said. 'She's RIGHT!'

Lizzie waited for her brothers to start protesting and complaining, claiming they'd never set such a challenge, but they didn't.

'HAPPY BIRTHDAY, Sis!' Milo smiled, while Isaac dug to the very bottom of the Lego box and pulled out a battered, old biscuit tin. He handed it ceremoniously to Lizzie.

Was this really happening? Was she dreaming? As she pulled open the lid, she was hit with the overwhelming smell of sugary flying saucers, popping candy, sherbet pips and liquorice worms. She was SPEECHLESS.

Then the three of them all climbed

up to the top bunk, snuggled under the duvet and shared the most magnificent midnight feast Lizzie could have ever wished for.

As she polished off the very last jellybean in the tin, Lizzie swore she'd NEVER be frightened of spiders AGAIN!

Busy Lizzie
and the
Very Pink Party

'This is a TOTAL disaster!' said Lizzie, speaking directly to Scuba, her toy shark, because there was no one else around.

One of her brothers had pushed an envelope under her bedroom door, and now she was shaking the sparkly, tiara-shaped invitation that had been inside in frustration.

'AARGHHH!' she howled, realising that she was causing glitter to hurtle off it in

all directions, and poor Scuba was now coated in a shimmering pink sheen.

The tiara-shaped invitation was an invite to her friend Sanam's VERY PINK PARTY.

The problem was that Lizzie HATED the colour pink. Just thinking about it made her feel like she'd bitten into an apple and discovered HALF a worm. Or she got that skin-crawling sensation like when her brother Milo SCRAAAPPPEEED his fork across his plate to make an ear-piercingly painful squeak (which he did JUST to annoy her). In fact, Lizzie was SCIENTIFICALLY ALLERGIC to the colour pink.

She knew that at Sanam's VERY PINK PARTY, there would be:

PINK decorations!

PINK face-painting!

PINK pass the parcel!

PINK princess songs!

PINK cupcakes!

PINK party games!

PINK prizes!

And, worst of all, everyone who was going would need to come in their loveliest PINK outfits!

What was Lizzie going to do?

Taking a deep breath, Lizzie marched across the school playground the next morning. She didn't like telling fibs, especially to her friends (brothers were a different matter), but this was an emergency.

Hanging upside down from the monkey bars, Sanam beamed and waved

to her. A little, fizzy knot of guilt formed in Lizzie's tummy. She bit her bottom lip.

'I can't wear pink,' she told herself. 'I just can't. I'm ALLERGIC!'

'Er... Sanam,' said Lizzie, 'I'm really sorry, but I can't come to your party tomorrow.'

'Why not?' asked Sanam, flipping the right way up, scowling so hard that her eyebrows almost met in the middle of her forehead.

'Um...' Lizzie gulped, looking around for an excuse. 'Er... er...'

Lizzie's eyes darted from one side of the playground to the other, then she caught sight of Year 4's display of garden insects.

'I've promised I'll look after my next-door neighbour's pet snail,' she blurted, before she could think of anything better.

'Bring the snail!' said Sanam, clapping her hands with excitement. 'In fact, the snail can be a special guest for Figgy, my new kitten. I can't wait for you to meet her. She's the fluffiest, cutest cat in the world.'

'Oh, I'd love to,' said Lizzie, her cheeks getting hot. (She really would. She ADORED cats, but not nearly as much as she HATED the colour pink.) 'But, er... I'm also in the grand final of a competition for scariest Halloween costume, so... er...'

'Lizzie, it's June!' Sanam pointed out. 'Halloween isn't for four whole months.'

'Oh, yeah. Of course, you're right. But I've also got to... um... match up all my socks!'

They both looked down at Lizzie's feet. She'd never worn a matching pair of socks in her life.

'Never mind,' said Lizzie, her heart sinking.

That evening, out of PURE desperation, Lizzie decided to ask her twin brothers for advice. They were ALWAYS getting out of things that they didn't want to do; they were basically PROFESSIONAL escape artists.

'PLEASE help me!' she begged, as Milo and Isaac noisily zapped zombie aliens on their computer.

'Get out of the way!' shouted Milo, annoyed, as Lizzie bravely stood in front of the screen, blocking their view.

'Only if you give me a perfect excuse for not going to Sanam's VERY PINK PARTY,' she said, digging her heels firmly into the carpet.

Even a cushion-missile pelted from Isaac didn't make her wobble. So, eventually, Milo groaned and threw down his controller.

'Blame us. Say you have to help tidy our room. If we don't, then Mum has threatened to cancel Christmas. SURELY Sanam will let you off then.'

Lizzie grinned. Yes, that would work. It HAD to.

Lizzie confidently searched the playground for Sanam the following morning, the excuse perfectly rehearsed in her mind. She looked in all the usual spots: under the little willow tree by the bike shed, around the corner from the water fountains, and at the very top of the climbing frame... but Sanam wasn't anywhere. Puzzled, Lizzie made her way to the girls' loos. Little whimpering sobs were coming from one of the cubicles.

'Sanam?' she called out, spotting a pink, sparkly school bag peeking out from under the door.

'The-The-d-d-door's not locked,' stuttered Sanam, between sobs.

Lizzie gently pushed open the door.

Sanam sat crumpled over a pile of soggy papers, her eyes red from crying.

'It's my kitten, Figgy. She's lost!' she said, still sobbing. 'I opened the window a crack when I was helping Mum bake all the pink cupcakes for the party, and Figgy must have slipped out. It's all my fault!'

She shoved a tear-soaked Lost Cat poster into Lizzie's hands.

'Oh, Sanam,' said Lizzie, putting an arm around her.

There was no other option, Lizzie realised with a heavy heart. She would HAVE to go to the VERY PINK PARTY and try to cheer Sanam up.

When Lizzie got home, she pulled open her wardrobe doors and stared at all the yellow and blue T-shirts, ripped jeans and navy jogging bottoms. She didn't have anything even a TEENY bit pink.

Searching through her drawers, she found some old tubes of paint. Before she could have a chance to change her mind, Lizzie squirted a huge dollop of red paint onto a crumb-ridden plate she'd found shoved under her bed. Next, she squelched out an enormous splat of white paint and determinedly mixed the colours together. PINK! The paint was suddenly very PINK! She swallowed hard, trying to stop herself feeling sick.

Standing in front of her mirror, she

decisively painted her shoes, trousers, T-shirt and hair all bright pink. Great long streams of paint dribbled down her forehead. She spun around to make sure she was totally covered. If poor Sanam wanted pink, then Lizzie would give her pink.

Now, Lizzie just had to sneak out of the house before her brothers saw her. She crept cautiously downstairs, leaving a trail of grubby, pink footsteps all the way to the front door. Just when she thought she'd got away with it, Milo spotted her.

'Isaac, come and see what Lizzie looks like!' he said, hooting with laughter.

Lizzie instantly felt her face get hot, and she knew she'd gone bright red.

'Her cheeks are as pink as her hair!' said Isaac, popping up from behind him. 'Get your phone!'

But before her annoying brothers got a chance to record her humiliation, Lizzie dashed out of the door. She was doing this for Sanam.

Sanam only lived two doors down, and as Lizzie reached Sanam's house, she narrowed her eyes. There weren't any PINK balloons tied to her gate. There were BLACK and WHITE ones, with pirate ships on the front. Several of her classmates were huddled excitedly outside the front door, waiting to go in. But they were NOT dressed in pink. Lizzie stared at the array of cutlasses, stripy tops and baggy trousers. Her eyes opened so wide that she couldn't even blink when Sanam pulled open the door. She had a toy parrot perched on her shoulder, and a skull and crossbones pinned across the front of her T-shirt. And not a patch of PINK in sight.

'Oh, Lizzie! I'm sorry. Didn't you get the message?' she asked. 'I told my dad  to text everyone. It's a pirate party now. Losing Figgy... it was because of all those horrible PINK cupcakes... I can't bear the colour any more.'

Lizzie watched as a big, fat tear trickled down Sanam's cheek. She felt so sorry for her friend, but she couldn't believe what she was hearing.

'Come on, everyone. Gather around for a photo,' said Sanam's dad.

Ten pirates all huddled together, waving cardboard swords and shouting 'Aye, aye, me hearties!'

There was NO WAY Lizzie was going to be in the photo. One pink, splodgy, painty figure in the midst of all those cool pirates.

Whilst everyone was scrambling into position, Lizzie skulked off into the garden. This was the WORST day ever. And Milo and Isaac were NEVER going to stop teasing her about it.

'Why had she painted herself pink?' Lizzie asked herself, annoyed.

She tried to scrape some of the pink out of her hair with her fingernails, but it was no use. It was completely matted in.

Angrily kicking the path, Lizzie stomped towards the shed. She would just wait in there till it was time to go home.

Suddenly, Lizzie heard a tiny little yelp. Cautiously, she creaked open the shed door and peered into the darkness. All at once, a fluffy little creature leaped into her arms.

'Figgy!' she said, stroking the little cat who was trembling all over. She carefully carried her back towards the house. When Sanam saw her, tears of relief streamed down her face.

'I can't believe you found her,' she said, hiccupping through her sobs. 'Thank you! Oh, thank you!' She hugged Figgy's soft, furry body up to her face.

'Well done, Lizzie!' said Sanam's dad. 'She must have got trapped in there. Thank goodness you found her.'

A lovely glowing feeling began to build inside Lizzie's tummy. In fact, she felt SO proud and pleased that she decided perhaps it'd be more fun to join in with the party games rather than just sulk.

And when Sanam's dad said it was time for a big game of Hide and Seek, Lizzie knew EXACTLY where to hide.
As Sanam counted slowly to ten, Lizzie charged upstairs and dived into Sanam's VERY PINK bedroom. She had pink curtains, a pink carpet, a pink bedspread, pink wallpaper and a pink lamp. Lizzie was COMPLETELY CAMOUFLAGED and was the very last person to be found.

52

'Perhaps the colour PINK isn't so bad after all,' Lizzie thought, as she was presented with her prize. The most enormous PINK box of chocolate she'd ever seen!

Busy Lizzie
and the Worst Weekend Ever

'YOO-HOO! Look at me!' Lizzie squealed, her flippered feet soaring through the air in an attempted reverse cartwheel.

She accidentally kicked over the fruit bowl, sending grapes flying everywhere, but somehow she landed triumphantly, with a banana perfectly balanced on her head.

Her twin brothers, Milo and Isaac, didn't even glance up. They just kept droning on about their new favourite video game.

'That noob only beat me because I was AFK,' said Isaac.

'Yeah,' Milo nodded, 'but at least we got revenge because I'm so OP.'

What were they even talking about? It sounded like another language!

Lizzie sulkily stomped into the living room. She'd ATTEMPTED to play Total Wreckage 3 with them, but they'd been furious at her for losing all their health points or something. It wasn't fair! Milo and Isaac shared a bedroom, and she bet they stayed up ALL NIGHT improving their skills on the computer. AND they probably had midnight feasts once Mum was asleep. Lizzie never had ANYONE to play with.

'It's Saturday,' Lizzie thought crossly. 'It SHOULD be the best day of the week!'

A happy, whooping sound drifted in from outside, so she stomped over to the window. Milo and Isaac were now in the garden, diving after a ball. She loved football, this was something she could join in with. So, she yanked off her flippers and raced to the hall to find her trainers.

'That's funny,' she thought. There was something stuffed in her trainer. She plunged her hand in and pulled out...
...A GIANT, HAIRY SPIDER!

'AARGHHH!' screamed Lizzie, dropping it as quickly as she could. Her brothers howled with laughter from the doorway.

'We got you, we got you!' laughed

Milo, picking up the spider and popping it in his pocket.

It was obviously plastic, Lizzie realised too late, as Milo and Isaac gave each other a giant high five and cheered, 'The Terrible Twins strike again!' in unison.

Lizzie was FURIOUS. Her brothers

loved playing pranks and had their own gang, The Terrible Twins. Unfortunately for Lizzie, she was always on the receiving end of their jokes. Only the other week, she was about to jump in the bath when she discovered hundreds of

BAKED BEANS floating in it. And last night, her bedtime hot chocolate had TOOTHPASTE on the handle and it smeared ALL over her pyjamas.

'That's it,' she decided. She was NEVER going to talk to her brothers again!

Lizzie charged up to her bedroom, slammed her door shut and wedged all her cuddly toys against it. Then she pulled out some paper, some coloured pencils and some glue from her desk. She'd decided she was going to write a book called *HOW HORRIBLE MILO AND ISAAC ARE.*

After ten minutes of scribbling away frantically, Lizzie heard yelling from downstairs.

'Who cares?' she thought. 'I'm not interested in anything my awful brothers are up to.'

Next, there was banging and clattering. Lizzie REALLY wanted to peep downstairs to see what was going on. But 'No,' she told herself firmly. It was probably just another one of their tricks.

Suddenly, there was a knock on her door. 'Lizzie, it's me. Can I come in?' asked Milo in a small voice.

'GO AWAY!' Lizzie shouted, but Milo pushed the door open anyway.

'What do you want? I'm busy!' said Lizzie, scowling, as she leaned over her work. Milo sidled into the room and flopped onto Lizzie's bed.

'It's Isaac! He's DESTROYED my best Pokémon card – the ultra-rare hologram one. I can't BELIEVE it! He said he'd been making slime for a prank, and it'd overflowed, going all over my card. AND apparently it's MY fault because I shouldn't have left the card on the table! I am NEVER going to forgive him! I can't share a room with him any more. Lizzie, can I move in here with you?'

'Hmm,' said Lizzie, considering the idea. She WAS mad at both her brothers, but only a few minutes ago she'd been feeling sorry for herself because she had no one to play with. And she'd ALWAYS wanted a room-mate.

'Pleeeaaassse, Lizzie! It'll be SO much

fun. We can stay up really late, and I'll play whatever games you want.'

'Even with my doll's house?' said Lizzie, narrowing her eyes.

'Anything! Please, Lizzie. I'm NEVER going to speak to Isaac again. I swear!'

'OK,' agreed Lizzie, leaping up and shoving her *HOW HORRIBLE MILO AND ISAAC ARE* book under her bed. 'What shall we do first? You choose. I can get out my dressing-up clothes, or we could make bracelets?'

'I need to move in all my stuff first,' said Milo.

Before Lizzie had time to think, Milo had whizzed out the door. There was a bit more banging and clattering. And a lot of shuffling. Then the door flew open again. Lizzie watched open-mouthed, as Milo dragged in:

his mattress

a gaming chair

a stack of books

three balls

a beanbag

a chest full of toys

a mountain of clothes

and 12 tins of Pokémon cards!

'Erm, is that everything?' said Lizzie nervously, as Milo stuck a HUGE football poster up over her bed. She glanced around. There was literally not a centimetre of floor space left.

'Oh well, it would be worth it tonight,' she thought, gleefully imagining the jokes they'd tell each other, the games they'd play and the secret snacks they'd scoff under the duvet by torchlight.

But at 9.12 p.m. that evening, Milo was SNORING loudly from his mattress on the floor. Lizzie flung her pillow at him.

'Come on! I thought we were going to stay up and tell spooky stories,' she hissed, but Milo just rolled over and started SNORING even louder.

Lizzie stared up at the ceiling. A stinky, cheesy sock smell wafted up from Milo's feet. She couldn't sleep. Why did she EVER want to share her lovely bedroom?

She needed to cuddle Scuba, her toy shark. He always made her feel better. So, she climbed out of bed to try and find him under all of Milo's things.

'OWWWEEE!' Lizzie yelped in pain, grabbing her foot.

Lizzie squinted in the darkness. Milo had insisted that she couldn't possibly leave her night light on. 'Night lights are for babies,' he'd said. That was all very well, but it wasn't Milo who was now standing on one of his precious Lego creations. She glared angrily at Milo's sleeping shape in the darkness. And then he let out an ENORMOUS, stomach-churning FART!

THAT WAS IT! She'd had enough sharing. Milo could toddle right on back to Isaac.

The next morning, Lizzie tried suggesting to Milo that perhaps he ought to forgive Isaac now, but Milo just held out the remnants of the treasured, slime-covered Pokémon card.

'Never!' he growled, crawling into HER bed and burying his head under HER duvet.

Lizzie wasn't giving up that easily. She went to find Isaac. He was in his bedroom, hanging from the top bunk with a drum around his neck. Music was blaring out at full blast as he tried to play along to his own beat.

'ISAAC!' yelled Lizzie as loudly as she could. 'YOU NEED TO MAKE UP WITH MILO.'

'No chance!' said Isaac. 'I LOVE having a room to myself. Milo never lets me near the top bunk or play my music. And now it's ALL MINE!'

He squeezed his eyes shut and nodded enthusiastically along to the music.

What was she going to do?

Back in Lizzie's room, Milo was still on her bed, happily flicking through one of her comics. Her cuddly toys had all been kicked to the floor, including Scuba the shark who had somehow turned up while she'd been gone.

'Don't you miss Isaac at all?' said Lizzie.

'No!' said Milo. 'You're a much better room-mate.'

Lizzie raised her eyebrows so high that they disappeared into her hair. Now she'd heard it all!

Milo grinned. 'Isaac always LEAVES his stuff everywhere, his feet STINK, he SNORES, and do you know what? He FARTS in his sleep!'

Lizzie rolled her eyes. There was only one option. She was just going to have to be THE WORST ROOM-MATE EVER so that Milo would be forced to go back to his old room.

That afternoon, while Milo was watching TV downstairs, Lizzie carefully put her plan into action. First, she set her alarm clock for 3 a.m. Surely that would annoy Milo. He had a table tennis tournament at school the next day and he wanted an extra-good night's sleep in preparation for it.

Next, she stuck flower stickers all over his football poster.

Then, she put on Milo's clean basketball kit. It hung down to her knees and it was ITCHY, but if it put Milo off wanting to share a room with her, then it was worth it. She picked up a glass of orange juice and accidentally spilt it down her front.

'Whoops!' she said, looking down at the spreading stain with delight.

Finally, she pulled apart all his treasured Lego creations and rebuilt them into a giant pirate-mermaid.

'Why are you wearing my kit?' Milo demanded, as he barged into Lizzie's room.

'Oh, is your show finished?' she asked innocently. 'I didn't think you'd mind now we're room-mates. I thought we shared everything.'

Lizzie smiled at him sweetly.

'Is that... ORANGE juice down the front?' said Milo. His face had started to go a very pale shade of purple.

Milo glanced at his poster and scowled. 'Are... are... are those FLOWER stickers?'

The pale purple was getting darker and spreading down his neck. Then he saw the Lego pirate-mermaid, and his face AND neck flushed the BRIGHTEST PURPLE Lizzie had ever seen. Milo spun around and stormed out of the room.

Oh dear! Had she gone too far? Was it going to be like that time she'd punctured all their footballs and she'd been GROUNDED for ages and ages?

Lizzie quietly shut her door... and waited.

A little while later, she heard Milo and Isaac calling her.

'Lizzie!' That was Milo. He still sounded a bit cross and, well, purply.

'Lizzie!' Now it was Isaac's turn. He sounded a bit cross too. Which was a little unfair as he didn't have anything to be cross about.

'Oh crumbs!' Lizzie thought. Were they both going to get her into trouble with Mum? She REALLY didn't want her pocket money to be stopped. She was saving up for rollerskates, and she'd already had the last five weeks' money confiscated for using up all Mum's spices when she was inventing magic potions.

Lizzie opened her bedroom door very slowly and crept into her brothers' room. She felt VERY nervous. And that wasn't helped by the fact that it was pitch black, except for a torch Milo was holding creepily under his chin.

'We've figured out what you're up to,' Milo said slowly as Isaac pushed the door shut behind her.

Lizzie gulped.

'You've been pranking me to try and make me move back in with Isaac.'

Lizzie's tummy flip-flopped over like a pancake made of jelly.

'I'm s-s-sorry,' she stuttered. 'I suppose you can stay in my room if you want, but...'

'...But you were brilliant!' said Milo, interrupting her mid-flow.

Now it was Isaac's turn to speak.

'We want to formally invite you to become an honorary member of THE TERRIBLE TWINS,' he announced.

'WHAT?' said Lizzie. This wasn't how she thought it would play out.

'You're a star pranker,' said Milo. 'First class! We could really do with you in our gang... especially as it's nearly April Fool's Day.'

'Oh! So, um, are you moving back in with Isaac?' asked Lizzie.

She'd said that he could stay in her room, but she hadn't really meant it. She needn't have worried though.

'Yep! I definitely am. I miss being on the top bunk,' said Milo, as Isaac handed her an official Terrible Twins badge.

Lizzie didn't know what to say as she pinned the badge on her top. She was now an official TERRIBLE TWIN! It wasn't often that she was lost for words, even if she did feel like pointing out that really the gang should now be renamed THE TERRIBLE TRIO.

Smiling, she walked proudly back to her room, remembering just in time that she needed to turn off the 3 a.m. alarm. Or the latest Terrible Twins prank would be on her. As usual!

Busy Lizzie

Makes a Difference

Lizzie was very much a CAN-DO sort
of girl, and even when things didn't go
completely her way (usually thanks to
her two older twin brothers, Milo and
Isaac), she tended to look on the bright
side. So, no one was more surprised than
Lizzie when dark clouds began gathering
over her happy world. It all started with
Sanam and the school play.

'I can't do it!' said Sanam, staring in horror at the school play script she'd just been handed. 'A solo! That means singing ON MY OWN... in front of EVERYBODY!'

'You'll be amazing,' said Lizzie, putting an arm around her friend. 'You have a beautiful singing voice. Like... Like... a penguin.'

Lizzie wasn't exactly sure what penguins sounded like, but she could tell Sanam was warming to the idea.

'AND you're going to be playing the part of a wizard. How cool is that?'

'But I haven't got a costume,' moaned Sanam, still unconvinced.

'You can borrow my starry dressing gown,' said Lizzie. 'And we can pour green glitter ALL over your hair.'

'OK,' said Sanam, with a little smile. 'I can't believe I have 33 lines to learn too. What part did you get, Lizzie?'

'Oh, um,' Lizzie looked down at her copy of the script. 'I'm... a... stick.'

She flicked through the stapled pages, searching hopefully for her name.

'I haven't got any lines,' she said eventually. 'I suppose sticks don't talk.'

Trying not to feel too disappointed, Lizzie trailed after Sanam, who skipped happily ahead to the playground.

In the playground, Lizzie spotted her big brother Milo slumped against a wall with his head in his hands.

'Milo, what's the matter?'

He may be mega-annoying, but Lizzie was genuinely concerned.

'I've been picked for the school basketball team and I'm SO nervous. I don't want to let my team down,' he said, staring at his feet.

'What? But you're BRILLIANT at basketball! The BEST! I bet you can land the ball in the hoop from the other side of the playground... with your eyes closed. AND while giving me a piggyback,' she added for good measure.

Milo's mouth broke into a grin. He could NEVER resist a challenge. So, Lizzie hopped on his back as he lined himself up. He squeezed his eyes shut and took aim. The ball soared through the air and glided perfectly through the hoop.

'Woo hoo! You did it!' said Lizzie. 'Now it's my turn. Bet I can do that too!'

She could feel herself beaming as she ran to pick up the ball. But when SHE threw it up in the air, the ball went the wrong way and bashed a hanging flower basket off the wall.

'Lizzie!' shouted the school caretaker. 'About time you went home,' he muttered, shooing her out of the school grounds.

Milo had made it look so easy. Why couldn't she get the ball even NEAR the hoop?

Lizzie trailed slowly after Milo as they made their way home together. Isaac, Milo's twin brother, must have gone home before them because she could hear his drumming all the way from the top of the road.

When Lizzie got into the house, she jumped around appreciatively, dancing to the beat of *We Will Rock You*. Once he'd come to the end of the song, Isaac put down his drumsticks and gave a long sigh.

'I just can't get it right, and the concert's tomorrow.'

'It doesn't matter, no one expects you to be perfect. You sound FANTASTIC!' said Lizzie.

'Yeah, you're right,' he said, surprising Lizzie by agreeing with her for once. 'It's all about the music after all, not the technical stuff.'

Then he bashed his drum set even louder.

'It looks like so much fun,' thought Lizzie. 'I wish I could play the drums!' But before Lizzie could ask Isaac for a go, her stomach started to growl hungrily. Where was Mum? It HAD to be dinner time.

She eventually found her mum huddled over her laptop, anxiously tapping away at the keyboard.

'Oh, hi, Lizzie,' said Mum, looking up with a smile. 'Guess what! I'm going to open a yoga studio and I'm trying to create an online advert for it. But I'm worried no one will sign up for my classes.'

'Mum, what are you talking about? OF COURSE they will!' said Lizzie. She'd seen her mum practising yoga in the front room. She was brilliant at it.

By now, Lizzie's tummy was grumbling SO noisily that you could probably hear it from Outer Space. But Mum looked way too busy to be thinking about dinner. And it was then that Lizzie had an idea. SHE could prepare a special surprise meal for her family to celebrate all their great news. Then she'd be too busy to think about her rubbish part in the play as a STICK or being USELESS at basketball or NOT having a drum set.

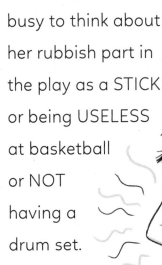

First, Lizzie set to work, cutting out little place cards for the table. All written with a glittery purple pen.

She laid them out on the table, then wrinkled her nose. Lizzie wasn't allowed to use the oven without Mum's help, so WHAT could she actually make to eat? She flung open the cupboard.

POTATOES!

ALL her family loved mash, and she'd watched Mum make it loads of times. How hard could it be?

She tried mashing four big potatoes in a bowl, but they were rock-hard. She even accidentally bent the fork. Lizzie was sure she'd seen Mum add milk to mashed potato. Maybe that was all she needed to soften them. Lizzie poured in a big glug, only to realise that she'd mistakenly added orange juice.

'Oh well,' she thought, shrugging. That would just give the dish a fruity twist.

She churned the potatoes around with a wooden spoon. It didn't really look anything like Mum's mashed potato, which was buttery and creamy and soft. What could she do?

Then Lizzie remembered they'd bought food colouring to make the icing for her

birthday cupcakes. Maybe she could mix
in some colours to make the potatoes
look a bit more appealing. Blue and
yellow makes... er... oh... GREEN! Lizzie
gave the bowl a hopeful stir. Perhaps
she'd invented an amazing new dish that
no one had ever thought of before. After
all, Mum was always saying she needed
to eat more greens.

Just then, the doorbell rang. It was Sanam. She'd come round to try on the wizard costume.

'Perfect timing! You can join us for dinner,' said Lizzie.

She quickly wrote out a little place card for her.

'Dinner's ready!' yelled Lizzie.

Sanam, Milo, Isaac and Mum all piled in around the table. But as Lizzie spooned out her VERY SPECIAL green potato dish, she didn't get quite the reaction she'd hoped for.

'Lizzie, you've used up ALL the orange juice!' said Mum, spying the empty carton lying on the side.

'Er... what's this?' asked Milo, looking at his plate with disgust.

'Um… it's very unusual,' said Sanam politely, as she scooped up a tiny dribble of green juice.

'Mum, we can't eat this!' said Isaac not so politely, attempting to jab his fork into a rock-hard potato.

'Never mind,' said Mum. 'All I care about is my clever family.' She looked around the table. 'Milo, I'm so proud of you, being picked for the school basketball team. And Isaac, I'm really looking forward to your concert tomorrow. And you too, Sanam,' Mum continued. 'That's great news that you got the part of the wizard in the school play.'

'What about your yoga studio, Mum? That's so cool,' said Milo.

'You know what,' said Mum, pushing her plate of green potatoes away. 'We have so much to celebrate tonight. Let's get a takeaway!'

Mum leaned back into a graceful yoga back arch and hooked a paper menu from a kitchen drawer with her toes.

Lizzie's heart sank. Whilst everyone was noisily debating whether to order pizza or Chinese, Lizzie sloped off miserably to the garden.

IT WASN'T FAIR! EVERYONE had something to celebrate apart from her. EVERYONE was good at something apart from her. She'd TRIED to make a special meal, but it had been a DISASTER!

Lizzie climbed up the rickety ladder to the old treehouse, but as she reached the top, the ladder crashed noisily down to the ground. Now, on top of everything else, she was stuck! Lizzie curled herself up into a little ball, feeling SERIOUSLY sorry for herself.

It was cold and lonely and quite spooky in the treehouse. Lizzie stared hard into the shadows. She was sure she could hear spiders whispering in the corners. They were probably planning a

giant party, to celebrate all their amazing web-making or something. And, of course, she wouldn't be invited. She'd even got a splinter from that horrible ladder.

Lizzie looked down at her hand which had started stinging. A big, fat tear rolled slowly down her cheek. No one even cared where she was. She was probably going to have to sleep out here. Maybe she'd have to live here FOREVER, and the only thing to eat would be cobwebs.

Suddenly, Lizzie heard voices calling in the distance!

'MUM!' she called, standing in the treehouse doorway. 'I can't get down!'

'Lizzie, what on earth are you doing up there?' Mum called back anxiously.

'Ouch!' she cried, as she tripped over the fallen ladder.

Mum leaned the ladder back against the trunk and clambered up to the treehouse, followed by Milo, Isaac and Sanam. They all squeezed into the tiny space and huddled around Lizzie.

'We've been looking everywhere for you,' said Sanam.

'What's the matter, Lizzie? What's going on?' said Mum, concerned.

'Everyone's good at something... apart from ME,' sobbed Lizzie, tears streaming down her cheeks and dripping off her chin.

She sniffed loudly. 'I can't sing. Or shoot basketball hoops. Or play the drums. Or do yoga.'

'Lizzie Boorman!' said Mum. 'YOU have one of the most magical, wonderful talents of all.'

'What?' said Lizzie, narrowing her eyes. She really wasn't in the mood for being told that she'd be just brilliant at playing a stick in the school play. Or that her meal was delicious after all. But Mum just carried on, smiling warmly at her.

'You just know how to make everyone feel better,' she said, giving Lizzie's shoulders a squeeze. 'When we're having a wobble, you steady us. When we're a bit unsure, you give us confidence. When we think we're rubbish, you make us feel fantastic. And you make me feel like the BEST yoga teacher in the world.'

Mum took a deep breath.

'Really?' said Lizzie in a little voice.

'REALLY,' said Milo.

'REALLY,' said Isaac.

'And making people feel good about themselves is actually the best talent ever,' said Sanam.

Lizzie bit her lip. Then she broke out into a giant toothless grin.

'I suppose you're right,' she said, as a warm, fuzzy feeling grew in her tummy.

Then it growled hungrily like an angry bear, making everyone laugh.

'Dinner time?' suggested Mum.

Lizzie nodded as Mum revealed an enormous takeaway box, with steaming hot pizza for everyone. They decided to stay up in the treehouse to eat, and happily fought over every last bite –

apart from the crumb Lizzie left for the spiders to enjoy. Surely even spiders like pizza.

AND it turned out that Lizzie's role as the stick in the school play was actually a PRETTY GREAT PART, because Lizzie wasn't any old stick. In the last scene, she turned into a magic wand and had to help save THE ENTIRE UNIVERSE! Now that was something worth celebrating!